PENGUIN MOON

written and illustrated by

ANNIE MITRA

Holiday House / New York

Library of Congress
Cataloging-in-Publication Data

Mitra, Annie.
Penguin moon.

Summary:
Penguin tries all sorts of things to get the moon to talk to him.
[1. Penguins—Fiction.   2. Moon—
Fiction.   3. Animals—Fiction]
I. Title.   PZ7.M69955Pe
1989   [E]   88-32797
ISBN 0-8234-0749-7

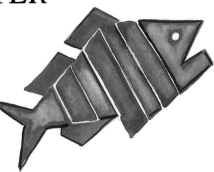

FOR *PETER*

On the icebergs, the nights were long
and the days were short.
Penguin liked to sit and look at the moon.
''I wish you would talk to me,'' he said.
But the moon was silent.

One night, Penguin asked the other penguins,
"Do you know if the moon can talk?"
"No, Penguin, we don't," they said.
"Why don't you ask Polar Bear?"

So Penguin went and found Polar Bear.
"Do you know if the moon can talk?" he asked.
"Go and ask Beluga," said Polar Bear.
"Can't you see I'm busy?"

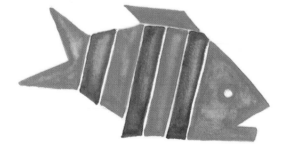

Penguin found Beluga playing with some dolphins.
"Excuse me," said Penguin. "Do you know if the moon can talk?"

"No, I don't," said Beluga. "But the giant starfish can tell you.
She knew the moon before she fell out of the sky."

So Penguin left in search of the giant starfish.

He swam and swam

and swam and swam

until he was far from home.

At last he found the giant starfish.

"I am the giant starfish that fell from the sky," she said.

She was very beautiful. Penguin bowed his head.

"What can I do for you?" she asked.

Penguin could hardly answer.

"I want the moon to talk to me," he said.

"I will let you wish five times
from each point of my star," said the starfish.

"If you're lucky, your wishes will come true."

Then she disappeared.

Penguin swam to the surface of the water
and climbed onto a big rock.
He waited until the sun set
and the moon was high in the sky.
Then he pointed his beak toward the moon
and began to wish really hard.
''I wish that the moon would talk . . .''

Before he could finish his wish,
a tiger appeared with a loud CRASH!
''Perhaps if I growl loud enough,
the moon will hear us,'' he said.
The tiger growled and roared all night
until his throat was sore.
But the moon did not talk.
And the tiger disappeared.

The next night, when the moon was high in the sky,
Penguin tried his wish again.
Before he could finish,
a kangaroo appeared with a big BANG!
''Perhaps if I hop high enough,
the moon will see us,'' she said.
The kangaroo hopped all night
until her feet were sore.
But the moon did not talk.
And the kangaroo disappeared.

On the third night, when the moon was high in the sky,
Penguin tried once more to make his wish.
Before he could finish,
an elephant appeared with a WALLOP!
''Perhaps if I flap my ears,
she will answer us,'' he said.
The elephant flapped his ears all night until they ached.
But the moon was still silent.
And the elephant disappeared.

On the fourth night, Penguin wondered if his wish
would *ever* come true.
But he decided to try one more time.
"I *really* wish that the moon would talk . . ."
This time there was a loud CRASH, BANG and WALLOP!
The elephant, kangaroo, and tiger landed
in a big heap in front of Penguin.
"We have an idea," they said.

"If we stand on each other's shoulders, the moon
will be sure to notice us."
So they climbed on top of one another until Penguin
was face to face with the moon.
"Now the moon can hear us," said Elephant.
"I wonder if she'll talk," said Tiger.
Suddenly the moon blinked.
Penguin held on tightly to Kangaroo.

"Hello, Penguin," said the moon.
  Her voice was deep and soft.
"So you *can* talk!" cried Penguin.
"Of course I can," replied the moon.
"You just couldn't hear me before.
  You weren't close enough."
"What's it like to live up in the sky?" asked Penguin.
"It gets lonely, but I like to watch you down there,"
  said the moon.

"Can you really see us?" asked Penguin.

"Yes, I can," said the moon. "What's it like down there?"

"I get lonely, too, but I have Polar Bear, Beluga,
and the other penguins to play with," said Penguin.
Penguin and the moon talked and talked
until the sun began to slowly rise.

"It's time for me to go," said the moon.
Penguin looked down. He missed his friends.

"I wish I were home," he said.

Suddenly Penguin was sitting on the icebergs.
The moon faded and Elephant, Kangaroo,
and Tiger disappeared.
Penguin's friends gathered around him.
"Well, can the moon talk?" they asked.
"Yes," said Penguin, "the moon can talk."

That night, Penguin sat on the icebergs
and looked up at the sky.
The moon flickered and glowed brightly.
The stars danced around her.
Penguin smiled and closed his eyes.
''Good night, Moon.''
''Good night, Penguin.''